Arrival

A wise report to a wise minister by a wise citizen

Hichem Karoui

Global East-West (London)

Contents

PART ONE: The Secret Report

V olumes in this series published by Global East-West (London)

Part One: The Secret Report

Part Two: Glorious Days in the Golden Age

Dedication

To the memory of Nana ...
Beloved mother...
You are always in my heart.
May you rest in eternal peace.

Mind Hacker

IN THE DARKNESS OF the night,
While I sleep,
I hear him tiptoeing in the corridor of my
mind,
trying to break into the Pyramid of my soul
and
steal memories, thoughts, projects,
time and space,
trying to control me,

to stop my run-up from the stars to Earth.

While sleeping,

I hear him

talking into my head,

betraying his unwelcome visit,

What a pretentious fool, falling out of resentment hell

is this?

Mind hacker...But

Mindless!

It's been years that you've been intruding,

You still did not understand?

You're getting nowhere,

I intercept you even before you reach the Gate of the Pyramid,

Do you still hope to get a piece of my soul?

Don't you understand I am the Pharaoh who came from the Future?

The living God who commands by telepathy,

The Eternal, with extraordinary over-reaching powers,

From a world that is far superior to yours...

Mind hacker...

Are you dumb?

Don't you see, for years, that you constantly failed?

You lost all your wars against me,

But you keep coming back,

And I keep locking you out of my Pyramid...

Who pushed you?

He who did lies to you,

He who did wanted you to fail,

And you failed,

Looser,

You obey failure,

That's why you're getting nowhere with me.

Mind hacker...

You are nobody,

Your power, if any, is limited by the Gate,

You have no key and no clue about my power.

Look at me,

I see you coming from millions of light-years,

You arrive creeping while I sleep,

You think I am unconscious,

You don't know the difference

between sleep and unconsciousness,

You live in a coma,

You hide,

You hope to snatch a piece of my soul

But you cheat yourself,

each time,

You will never wake up...

Do you still expect me to allow you in the domain of the sacred soul?

You don't know me,

You spent your life trying to find the Gate of the Pyramid,

And you still get locked out,

How can you pretend to know?

You are a lost dog in the desert,

Bark: yap, yap!

Bark: yap, yap, yap!

Bark again
and again, you lose,
What a shame!
Are you then ignorant or powerless?
Mind hacker...
I am the Pharaoh from the Future who built
that Pyramid up,
I am the God of certainty and uncertainty,
I am the light and the dark,
The sun and the moon,
The clay and the wind,
The water and the fire,
I am the Forefather of Adam,
I came from the stars when your earth was a
baby-planet with no human being around,
I saw the birth of the first man,
The first woman,
I was born in the Future,
I have no limit in time and space,
Mother and father were the terminals that
allowed me to land on Earth.

Mind hacker...

You pretend to know me

You don't even know yourself,

You have no face,

I have many,

You have one voice,

I have millions,

Did you ever try to recognise the truth of your

non-existence?

That, you cannot.

Deprived as you are from life and conscious-
ness.

Mind hacker...

When you come back tonight,

or tomorrow,

or the night after,

Look at me again,

Maybe you will understand that

on earth, you have no way to reach me,

Come back with the troops,

Let them be armed to the teeth,

Try to penetrate the Pyramid again with the army,

With aircraft and armada,

Maybe,

Maybe you could dig a little hole in the wall,

enough for the Pharaoh to bury you,

Because, as you now know,

You have no way against me.

Mind hacker...

Did you get it now?

I am the spaceman,

My home is the Cosmos,

The multi-universes are my domain,

I am not related to you, nor you to me,

Don't try to create a connection,

There is none between us,

There will never be,

You are already dead,

You belong to the past,

I belong to the Future,

Mother and Father came to earth with a mission:

They delivered me
and returned to the Future,
They are still there,
Watching me, watching us.
I am the Next man,
The Future of Humanity,
You are dead past,
I am endowed with a Cosmic Supermind,
You have no idea what it is,
On earth, I am the Master,
I control the controller,
I command you, mind hacker,
From the deepest point in the universe,
From inside the Pyramid of my soul.
Mind hacker...
Get lost... with your resentment,
You belong in Hell!

16 September 2022

Notes

The Publisher

This is Mister Bassam Bourasin's admitted report as a citizen of His republic. He didn't give it a name. He originally addressed it to the Interior Ministry. Instead, it landed on my desk. I publish it as is, with no major changes to its form or content. However, because the report is around 800 pages long, it will be serialised. The first book, Arrival, can be found here, and others will be added soon. I should also point you that this is a translation. The first draft was written in Arabic.

The author had no intention of publishing it. In any case, it is understandably unpublishable in the country... for the same reasons that silence any samizdat.

Hichem Karoui

The Author

ALL OF THE INDIVIDUALS in my story, as well as the country, are not made up. However, even if some characters claim to be more fictive or strange, crazy or foolish than others, they are not required to justify their

location. My country can be found throughout the Arab world. Whatever name people
give it, you won't notice a difference if you pay
attention.

Bassam Bourasin

"Nobody did a secret deal,

Nobody was for sale,

Nobody bent the rules at all,

And nobody went to jail,

And all of them were honest men,

As white as driven snow,

And lived on a higher plane,

And shat on those below..."

Roger Woddis: All Clear

"And so, what could my sterile and uncouth genius beget but the tale of a dry, shrivelled, whimsical offspring, full of old fancies such as never entered another's brain — just what might be begotten in prison, where every discomfort is lodged and every dismal noise has its dwelling?"

Cervantes: Don Quixote (Prologue)

Chapter One

A pril

I've always hated this city. I just got here two days ago. I walked into what appeared to be a guesthouse. A darkish man hurried through the lobby. Smiling. Reeling. Drooling like a puppy who has discovered a bone. The reception has taken me by surprise. Too warm to be genuine.

Furthermore, I had never seen him before. I didn't have any baggage. He didn't inquire. He scribbled my name and location. I inquired as to where I would spend the night. He raised his head, glanced at me, and murmured, "Upstairs, sixth floor." There is enough space for everyone.

I was thoughtful. I gave him a tip. At his request, I gave him the coins in my pocket. He demanded more. Wallet. Tie. Shoelaces, too.

I'm not sure if I took the elevator or walked the stairs.

The fog encased my memories like a dream.

I WAS SOON ON THE SIXTH story of that strange building, which is merely one of the numerous compounds that make up the large hotel. I am still hazy. I'm having trouble recalling every moment of my arrival. People in this town mistaken me for a dangerous individual. A kind of buccaneer, if not a terrorist, plotting the destabilisation of the STATE. Not all, however. The shrink, the black guy at the front desk, and my angels.

Each person, according to an old Islamic belief, possesses two angels. One observes and even advises. The other is a bookkeeper. He keeps track of our good and bad behaviours from the moment we are born until the day we die. As a result, on the last judgment, they give the material to the Boss. Following that would be either a reward or a penalty. My angels are not pleased with my behaviour, and I know this. This is a different story, which I will continue later.

I was rather taken aback at the time. Even a little perplexed by the bizarre situation I found myself in. I was on the sixth floor of this weird structure. I arrived there in the same way that one penetrates the substratum of a false dream. The scene that appeared in front of my eyes was more than spectacular.

It was a stretched platform on which people sat on their beds, much like in ancient inns. Hem! Excellent inns? I'm probably exaggerating a little. No, it was quite the opposite. I mean, there was no privacy, no intimacy, nothing. Everyone could see and hear what the next-door neighbour was doing. It was so promiscuous! I was taken aback. It should go without saying. That, however, is not the point.

I shifted my head to the right, and what I saw next stunned me. People were piled up and parked like cattle in a kind of chamber with a basin full of nasty brown water in the centre. Hundreds of people arrived for no obvious reason save for the pool, where they could hardly bathe, as I estimated. I approached the long ribbon that separated them from the rest of the platform with caution, startled. One of them exclaimed, "Mind the border!" Did I go too far? Some looked at me as if I were a strange beast from another planet rather than a human person like them. I was slightly embarrassed by their eyes examining me and scrutinising my face, clothes, and overall appearance. It would be inaccurate to suggest that it did not worry me. I kept saying out loud: "What's the problem? What's the matter with me?" I almost forgot that the anomaly was not in my circumstance but rather theirs. Because it was obvious that they were being held in custody...

As the borderline was guarded by two guys in grey uniforms, they couldn't walk freely - like me, I imagined - and leave the hotel anytime they wanted. For a little period, I stood by the ribbon. Mesmerised. I overheard the conversation. It was a genuine Babylon!

I couldn't comprehend everything but felt they weren't talking about philosophy or scientific breakthroughs. I pondered what had brought all those men together on the outskirts of that filthy pool on the sixth level of that weird hotel! I was astounded by their sight and nearly revolted by how they crowded together like a herd of domestic animals. Their position was out of the ordinary and depressing. Then I suddenly realised that, unlike them, I was free, and I kept repeating to myself: "I am, indeed, a free man. He's free, free, totally free..."

IF THAT HAD BEEN A dream, I would have awoken sweating and gasping for oxygen. But, because I didn't, I must own that what seemed to me at the time to be a terrifying but fleeting nightmare has now become - alas! - the truest and singular reality. Even yet, as

I compared myself to those wretched captives and realised that I was in a different situation (I could still go fast, couldn't I?) I had no idea why, out of all the hotels in town, I had to stay in that one. Indeed, I did not select it, but who does? As far as I recall, I was always told that one should never select what one does in life because everything is already Mektub! Before we are born. The holy pen has already written all that will happen to us, from the cradle to the grave. And as everything is Mektub, it is meaningless to ponder why I am here or there or even why I am writing this down right now. I honestly don't know. That is also precisely what I said when one of those guys questioned me. He didn't appear convinced by my response. He looked at me almost obnoxiously, possibly trying to find the deception in my features.

HE WAS A YOUNG MAN with brown

hair. About 36 years old. Brown skin tone. A large brow. His large specs make his eyes as small as a mouse's. I'm not sure why I thought of a mouse instead of a cock or a cat. Perhaps because he also had a narrow face, two small ears, a long-pointed nose with large nostrils and tufts of hair in the cavities, and dry and thin lips. Perhaps because, unlike me, I thought he was imprisoned in that cage like a mouse. Anyway, since he was the first to address me and seemed irritated by my response, I decided not to chastise him. So I added an explanation:

- I'm simply a visitor passing through.

- A visitor! He repeated, either mockingly or amazedly.

- Yes, I replied. Why are you so taken aback?

- Oh, please, my friend. I'm not. I've seen others who came to visit, just like you! They were so thrilled that they preferred to stay with us! They are still present.

When he sensed my amazement, he chuckled. Then he took my elbow gently and asked:

- Come along, pal, will you? Just don't go over the line. We can talk. We have plenty of time... I explained that I needed to find a room.

- I can't stay the night in this filthy place. I need to speak with the lobbyist...

- Don't, he yelled. They'll assign you to us. Do you see the mud? If we're fatigued, we can't even sit down, lie down, rest, or do anything...
- Why? So, are you punished?

- Of course, my friend, we are. Purgatory is what they call it. And then there's hell, which is far more sinister. They say it's the freezer!

I was concerned. I began to wonder whether I hadn't entered a mental institution. Some other males began clustering around us and listening to what we were saying. They were all pitiful, clad in filthy rags, with sunken unshaven cheeks and goggling, weary eyes. Despite their terrible misery, they were nonetheless interested in what I had to say! I suppose any newbie would provide them with amusement. It was as if I were conveying the last news from a world that had been barred to them for months, if not years. Because all eyes were on me, I began to feel more significant than I had ever thought of myself. I anticipated dozens of questions popping up in their heads and lips. I was spruce in comparison. I had just arrived at that hotel, pompously dressed in a blue suit - the holiday suit - with a bright white shirt, and although I was untied, my elegance was still intact.

The Administration's wisdom became evident to me at that point. Customers must entrust the reception desk with their encumbering accoutrements, such as money, wallets, ties, laces, and so on, as soon as they come... The wise Administration is cautious and preventive, knowing very well the type of services its home is showing and entirely responsible for the tranquillity of its clients. A tie and a good lace may complement a plain dress perfectly, which is as convenient as agreed upon. Nonetheless, in some instances, they may be used as dangerous weapons, either to kill someone or to commit suicide.

Any good hotel that cares about its reputation would not let its customers die under its ceilings if they could avoid it. That is precisely why this hotel is concerned about the safety of its guests. SECURITY is even the buzzword here! And they are correct. Because one cannot live in peace if they are not secure. And if one cannot live in harmony, the only option is to leave. It is evident that no hotel in the world wants its clients to depart because they do not feel safe; my hotel is no exception. Furthermore, the hotel's administration is so devoted to its guests that as soon as they register your name, they ask you to forget it. Another stumbling block! What generosity! What shrewdness! What brilliance!

They understand that no one picks their name freely because we are all baptised by our parents. As a result, mindful that clients may become tired of a word they will have to live with for the rest of their lives, they provide you with an excellent service. Indeed, which is unavailable in other hotels: it is to forget your name at least during your stay in this welcoming abode. Instead, they would assign you a number, such as 1007, as your new name. Isn't that a simple and pleasant thought? Naturally, it is. However, it is not for everyone.

WHEN I WAS CONVERSING with that person - I mean the mouse - I closely watched the people around me. Many of them were ut-

terly unknown to me. I dare to say the majority
was what some call the mob, sometimes with
scorn. I read a lot about it, especially in my
old newspapers, magazines and school manu-
als, which I maintain in my archives. That is
not a pedantic statement. I had no idea what
this last word meant until I looked it up in
the dictionary. But I'm getting away from the
point. This is not acceptable to me. So I stated that among the faceless faces of the mob, I
thought I recognised some very familiar things.
They were, after all, on our daily media menu
until recently. Men of renown, political and
financial luminaries. I'm referring to the Old
World before its demise due to the coup revolution that elevated our beloved General President (BGP) to absolute authority. I only state
that the names those men bear from the cradle to the grave are likely to be more significant and less tedious than those of ordinary
mortals. As a result, I conclude that they must

be dissatisfied with being reduced to uncertain numbers. I don't suspect the Administration of malice; such thoughts are foreign to me. I've been taught to trust my hierarchical superiors and the Administration throughout my career. Their excellent intentions and dedication to the country's highest interests are unquestionable. I'm not going to change my mind right now. That would be absurd at my age and in my situation. I am trustworthy, and my devotion to the Administration is unquestionable

···Hem! At the very least, it should be. That's why I've lived in royal tranquillity for the last twenty years. (There's no need to say "royal". Just say, "in peace." OK!) I am not, by definition, a troublemaker. My angels are now giggling, and I challenge them to find any evidence that I am lying. Knock!

Chapter Two

For nearly two decades, I was a respected citizen in my country. I was so dedicated to my career and my bosses that I rarely left the city without their permission. I didn't want to be misunderstood. I was always informed that the Capital is the site of various conspiracies and wicked machinations. A good bank clerk is expected to stay where he is assigned to work. As long as I could, I never strayed from this promising path. Oh! Perhaps it would be more honest to admit that I visited the Capital. As a result, I am not a complete novice. But because I wasn't alone, I wasn't trespassing. The bank did send me here with other employees, and I didn't care for the city. I wish I hadn't been here so long. That concerns me. However, because the Administration has approached me, it is up to them to decide for me. I will not get involved since it's none of my business. Anyway, I'm not alone, as usual.

I noticed that Mister Aroussi, the bank's Director, had arrived before me. On the far side of the pool, I noticed him cheerfully conversing with a group of well-known Old World politicians. He, like everyone else, had his necktie and laces removed. He would not, however, commit suicide. He is too optimistic to give up hope in bettering the human condition, and it is pretty unlikely that he will assassinate someone coldly.

A man of integrity, truly. It was the first time I had seen him dressed so casually. He must have also obtained his phone number. Certainly, that is reason enough for him and me to rejoice. Nothing is more valued by us - bank employees - than the immense satisfaction of being transformed into numbers, isn't it? That is the proper reward for a successful career in the service of numbers. A long-held secret desire: to be or not to be a number. That is the query! I dare to say it's miraculous for any bank clerk's worth of work. My employer, on the other hand, must believe he is in heaven. The answer is simple: he has a considerably longer career in the numbers service than I do. Fortunately, the unfortunate old man received his award before retiring. I'll congratulate him as soon as I can contact him.

- HAVE YOU SEEN THE shrink? - inquired the man with whom I was conversing.

- No, sir, I said. I've never seen a therapist in my life. I'm not insane, Alhamdu Lillah.

- Nobody told you you were, my friend. A trip to the shrink is mandatory in this town. All newbies are eventually summoned to his office.

- Are you sure? For what purpose? Are we also suspected of insanity?

- Maybe! He paused for a bit before saying, - Look here, my friend. I'll give you some sound counsel. Are you ready to take it?

- Well... The other men drew a tighter circle around us.

- Listen up: when they take you to the shrink, he'll ask you certain things about your private life that you may find embarrassing, such as your childhood, parents, family history, and possibly your political and religious beliefs. Then pretend to be a fool.

- Could you please excuse me?

- Play the fool, he exclaimed forcefully, grinning and gesticulating ludicrously.

The others burst out laughing, and some of them imitated his mime. I glanced at them, astounded and perplexed.

- I'm not a fool, I said.

- We fucking know you aren't, one of them yelled. It's nothing more than a ruse.

Another said:

- It was to defraud the shrink.

I cleverly inquired:

- Why should I play that comedy?

- Otherwise, the shrink will think you're intelligent enough to be thrown in with the monsters of purgatory or a tiny dark pit in the freezer. Then you'll be in so much trouble that you'll curse your damned I.Q. and wish you were just bloody stupid. Do you understand now?

- Hell! I burst out laughing. But I don't consider myself brilliant in any case. Sir, I'm merely a bank teller. I'm not looking for trouble.

I truly meant it, but no one seemed to believe me.

- As you wish, responded the man with the big glasses. But don't tell me you weren't warned.

"Asshole!" I heard behind me. I felt a little guilty, so I said aloud:

- Okay! I'll do my best.

- That's wise, he said.

Nonetheless, I was completely mortified. Was it essential to make a fool of myself to find calm in this place? Apparently, the man understood my mind because he added:

-Look here, my friend. All of those who have been granted some comfort around here are not particularly bright, but they play the game. Do you understand? We in purgatory are already doomed because we are labelled "politicians." Do you know what this means right now in this country? So, here's my recommendation: Be intelligent and astute. Accept being an idiot in front of the shrink. If you're lucky, you'll win.

Lucky? To be sure, that's what I am.

Chapter Three

The shrink, on the other hand, was not what I expected. I have no idea why he was labelled a "shrink." When the lobby attendant led me to the first-floor office, I noted that "Social Assistant" was written on the gate.

My guard, a gorilla masquerading as a robust black middle-aged man clad in a dirty grey uniform tightly encircled his large fat body, told me to wait. They will call me. I nodded and thanked him profusely for his help. But he was in a bad mood that morning as curses poured out of his mouth, and I feared he would knock me down. I dashed up to the people gathered near the shrink's gate and flung myself among them, hoping for some safety. But it was the wrong thing to do. Those who had been waiting before me for a long time were not pleased. They booted my bottom and pushed me out of the row, possibly believing I was attempting to impress them with my privileges as a respected bank employee, which never occurred to me. The black man watching the situation became enraged once more and yelled:

- Ho! You fucking shit-brain bastard! Piss off before I ruin your horrible facade.

I apologised and began to explain that I was not looking for trouble. Nonetheless, I was interrupted by another kick in the shin. I crept on all fours and hurried to the back of the row. Everyone was laughing. I got to my feet and stood behind them, humbly apologising again. It wasn't exactly what you'd call a successful entrance. As far as I recall, my august buttocks had never been booted so badly by any foot. However, one must gain experience; everything begins with a beginning. I've already said that the welcome in the foyer was far too warm to be genuine. So now I have grounds to believe I was correct. Nonetheless, I must admit that my awkwardness was the actual cause of the unfortunate situation. If I was so clumsy, the cause isn't difficult to guess: I had a terrible, almost white night.

I HAD SCARCELY CLOSED my eyes. Not only was there not a single empty room on the sixth floor but there were no rooms at all. Disabused, I decided to leave that crowded, pitiful place and hunt for better accommodation elsewhere. However, I discovered that the gate had been closed. As a result, I had no choice except to stay with the gang and find a couch. Unfortunately, that was an impossible assignment because all of the beds were full, and many were even sleeping on the floor. I stumbled through the place, pacing back and forth, looking for a spot to sleep. Because of all the bodies carpeting the ground, even walking became difficult. So the prospect of spending the night splayed out on the cement felt unimportant, upsetting, and unworthy of a bank clerk. I stood up in the middle of the room, embarrassed. I had no idea the hotel would be that congested.

Nonetheless, this is a well-liked home. Later, I discovered that some consumers visit for the second, third, or tenth time. Even better, several of them claim to have made over thirty visits! How can you not admire them? Such devotion is an indication of outstanding moral character. It merits respect, especially when one knows that the risk of spending several white nights on the cement is always present. I have always admired faithful men regardless of the subject of their attachment. I am utterly loyal to the Administration—not just the bank, but The Administration, the Big One.

Nevertheless, despite my adoration and respect, I couldn't bring myself to lie down on the floor like them. Not to dismiss the behaviour, but I believe it is irrelevant for a bank clerk to degrade himself skittishly by being unaware of his position. In a nutshell, it was demeaning. So I remained proudly steadfast. I had not ignored the community, nor was I unaware of my status. A bank clerk is someone of some social standing, perhaps the most significant. Consider how our modern society would be without banks! It would devastate the state's civilian and military institutions.

Where would consumers be able to get a better deal for their money? Who would look after their deposits and earnings? Where might the government and investors look for funding for their projects? Who else can support development objectives and provide a solid foundation for the national budget? Isn't it true that banks are at the centre of the economy? Can we define a state that does not have an economy? - That is a callous state. Who would want to live in such a state? Certainly not me. Furthermore, if this is true for states, it is also true for families. Everyone should be grateful to banks, especially bank clerks, for assisting us. Thus, once the value of banks is recognised, it is clear that they are worthless without their clerks. As a result, bank clerks should be recognised as the most helpful kind of public servants. More valuable than cops, more valuable than troops, teachers, doctors and chemists, and even ministers and...(STOP! Hem!) May be... Indeed not the ministers.

I AM NOT, IN FACT, flattering myself. For example, when a consumer visits the bank for the first time, who else but the bank clerk can guide him through the maze of accounts of numbers, accounts of numbers, and accounts of numbers?

And who else looks after the customer's pocketbook and interests while he is extremely busy and away from his deposits, whether at home or abroad, and discovers numerous ways to make him prosper?

As a result, just as our modern civilisations cannot reject and survive the banking system, the banking system cannot refuse the clerks and outlive them. They are analogous to the heart and arteries that transport blood - or money - through the social body. As a result, the bank clerk is the main artery of the economy. If you cut that artery, you short-circuit any sound and healthy life in the country. Do that if you want havoc and anarchy. Do it right now. Take note of how sensitive I am. It is neither wise nor prudent. That is something that a good administration should be aware of. (However, I'm digressing and messing with policy here.) When I trespass, as usual, a red light notifies me. The final sentence, for example, is to be removed. I don't want to be mistaken for someone who advises or criticises governments on policy. It is not my intention).

AS I HAVE THE MOST gratifying honour of being your humble servant and an artery transmitting what should be sent to the heart of our country, I am conscious that the immense importance of my bank has strengthened my modest original condition.

So I couldn't lie down on the floor without jeopardising my institution's good name. As a result, I was willing to give up my right to relax for the benefit of my bank.

Alas! You know how weak human nature is! When the sun rose, I heard the black guard calling my name. To my astonishment, I opened my eyes to find myself strewn down the floor! I almost cried because of the treachery. What a pity!

Chapter Four

The shrink - I'll use the same name as the clients for consistency - is a small white-haired, black-eyed man of around fifty years old, with silver-rimmed glasses falling over his prominent nose, a wide mouth, and a hoarse voice. When his aide led me into his office, I saw him smoking a cigarette. He cast a sidelong glance at me through a cloud of blue smoke before plunging his gaze listlessly into his papers. I assured myself that this was a heavy smoker. Furthermore, the ashtray on his

desk was overflowing with butts. When the assistant saw it, he rushed to empty it into the basket   before
l   e   a   v   -
ing.

- Please sit, the gruff voice said after a moment.

I did this while thanking him for his generosity. The office was not particularly large. There was no carpet installed on the floor. Except for a framed portrait of our Beloved General President (BGP), which was hung just above the head of the shrink across from the gate, the walls were bare. To the left and right were two large glass-panelled closets with many arrayed folders on their shelves. A solitary window illuminated the iron bars. I could only stare at the uniformed guys swarming about the courtyard, where many police vans were parked.

Of course, I was taken aback by their sight. Except for watching official events on television, I have never seen so many police officers and security guards. That was supposed to mean, "be careful!" This hotel has several VIPs, which surely benefits its reputation and tourism.

The shrink began reading my file:

- Mr. Bassam Bourasin...

I thought it would be appropriate to begin with a good joke. I interrupted, saying:

-Yes, sir, my buddies nickname me "BB" or "baby", and laughed. Did you notice anything? Brigitte Bardot and I share the same initials.

He didn't even crack a smile. Instead, he gave me that lethargic, listless look I had noticed on my entry. It felt as though my existence was unimportant to him. When I left his office, he forgot my name, face, and everything about me! I didn't blame him. He is so solicited and preoccupied with all the patients waiting outside. As a result, it was obvious that he would not recall everyone. However, it is undeniable that I deserved particular consideration as a bank clerk.

He said:

- Mister 1007, your name is Bassam Bourasin. You are a 39-year-old bank worker who is a bachelor and lives in 'Ouja. Is that correct?

- Hem! Certainly, sir.

- You've been with 'Ouja Bank for around fifteen years, which is a long period. What caused you to get into trouble?

- There isn't any cause, sir. I wasn't looking for problems. I am a responsible citizen, and...

- You were, he stated emphatically. I'm sorry, but I read dreadful charges in your file. Corruption, fraud, various and recurring swindles, affiliation with criminals, offending authorities, and, last but not least, monarchism! Otherwise, a counter-revolution activity! Hell! If only three of these charges are proven to be accurate, you will be sentenced to twenty years in

prison, which is more than your whole banking career. Do you realise this?

- Sir, yes. Hem... Of course, sir, I mean no.
These allegations are false. Indeed, I don't want
to insult the cops by dismissing them as lies.
Nonetheless, I've worked without complaint
for nearly a quarter-century. Sir, my hands
are as white as snow. Even when I merited
it, I never expected a reward. Millions in all
known currencies have passed through my fingers. Never, I said, never did I feel... never did I
fancy... never, even in my dreams, did I think it
might be mine. Throughout my long service,
I've had numerous opportunities to steal the
safe and go to Europe or possibly America. It
wasn't difficult because my boss and coworkers
trusted me. So, why should I abruptly change
my mind and end up in hot water? I am a
trustworthy citizen. After the Central Bank,
my bank is one of the most important in the
country. Everyone in my small town respects

me. Hem! I was! I believe I am still fairly compensated. I have nothing to be upset about. Furthermore, I do not have a wife, children, or other familial responsibilities that would pressure or drive me insane, leading me astray from the right path. No, sir. I wasn't even able to spend my entire salary. I was saving to live a comfortable life in my old age. As a result, I purchased a lovely little flat in my hometown, and I am still paying its monthly instalments. I was...um... I'm still planning to marry an honest 'Ouja girl. In a nutshell, sir, I am content. Why should I give up my happiness or trade it for some erratic delusions?

He lit another cigarette and looked at me through the blue smoke. The gruff voice continued, coldly and detachedly:

- Well, you asked the appropriate question. Give me the proper answer now.

- Would you like the truth, sir? The whole truth?

- Of course, yes.

- Rumours, slanders, and nonsense!

- I beg your pardon.

- Sir, you heard me. These charges you read to me are complete fabrications.

- That's what you'll have to prove in court.

"Because there will be a trial as well!" I was going to reply, but he interrupted me and asked:

-In the meanwhile, how can I help you?

Such generosity relieved and emboldened me to the point that I pleaded:

- Get me a comfortable room where I can have some solitude, please.

For the first time since I'd seen him, he appeared to smile. That, though, lasted only a second or two.

- If I were you, I wouldn't say that, he said. But, you know, up here, privacy usually means the freezer.

My blood froze when I heard that word. But before I could respond, the shrink continued:

- It's not a first-class hotel, Mister 1007, but a prison, I'm afraid.

He couldn't be more terrified than I was, and most of all, disappointed by his candour, I stuttered something along the lines of:

- It wasn't necessary to use this... abominable word... I ... I...

He cut me off abruptly:

- I realise you're hypersensitive, but you'd better confront reality 1007. You've been arrested and heavily charged. You must account for everything you do inside and outside these walls. Now, if you have any questions, please let me know. I'll forward it to the administration.

- Yes, sir, I responded thoughtfully and gently. I am ready to confront reality. I'm ready to go home.

FINALLY, I CAN SAY that the visit to the shrink was not all that horrible. I didn't go home, nor did I obtain a private room. He urged me not to make any more "foolish assertions." Nonetheless, I received critical compensation. He secured me a job at the library instead of the hotel's bank, either because he was moved by my case or because he wanted to put me to the test.

- Look, Bassam, he said.

That was unusual and awkward of him. He disobeyed an important prison rule by using my first name instead of my barcode. If he hadn't been so gracious, I'd have to report this infraction to the administration. I'm not going to do it. So we're calling it quits. But wary of any deviations next time...hem!

He said:

- I see you are a one-of-a-kind nature! You're so well-intentioned that I'm afraid you won't get through the fight with the ravenous sharks over here. So, I'm willing to help you, but you must vow to be obedient and serious.

- I assure you, sir.

- We require assistance at the library. Do you enjoy reading?

I eagerly responded:

- I enjoy reading, sir. I'll treat their pages with the same care as banknotes.

He coughed slightly and remarked:

- Very good. The task is straightforward: inmates would borrow books, and you would receive them and make the process simple.

- As in a bank, sir...

- Yes, but it is a learning experience. We'd like them to read books. Is this clear?

- Exactly, sir. I'm not going to ask for any loan guarantees...no mortgages, no real estate, no properties, nothing. I'm not deaf; I regard it as educational. Nonetheless, I must caution you against making such a fatal error.

He was perplexed and questioned:

- What do you mean?

- I mean, if you offer people everything they want without repercussions, your library will become bankrupt instantly. Indeed! You'll need money to pay for maintenance, services, and new books, sir. Where are you going to look for it?

He looked at me as if he was discovering my existence for the first time. Whoop! I assured myself that I was becoming someone in his eyes. Then I noticed him crossing his hands, which reminded me of anxiousness - or impatience? His expression darkened somewhat as he looked at me, and he uttered his words as though rescuing himself from the grip of rage:

- That's none of your business, he replied dryly. Should I consider you a damned fool?

I was perplexed. Is there anything I said that was incorrect? However, he appeared to have overcome his rage, for after a while, he whispered:

- Sorry! You're probably correct. Your remark demonstrates that you are a cautious and astute individual.

But... At that point, I became panicked since I remembered the guy's warning in purgatory. Then, with increasing confusion, I realised the shrink was probably testing me and that I had fallen, hands and feet tied into his trap. I realised I needed to act quickly. So I interrupted him and said:

- No sir, no! I'm afraid you're mistaken...

He stared at me, perplexed. I said:

- I am neither cautious nor cunning, as you imagine. I am even below average in intelligence... Sir, I mean below... far below. My mother used to say, "You're a carbon duplicate of your father, boy!" ... Yes, a duplicate of my father; and my father... Everyone knows he was a knucklehead, sir. You'd never say if he's incredibly intelligent or stupid. He could be both at the same time; it was his privilege. But I'm not going to mislead you by claiming that he left me the brightest part of his magnificent mind. I'm not sure.

It appeared to work. The shrink looked at me for a long time, then lit another cigarette and went smoking.

- My son, you're a strange phenomenon! He stated.

- Sir, I am a stranger in this town.

- Are you a stranger? Yes, if you put it that way. If your father's description is incorrect, you're in big trouble. Even if it is correct, you may suffer from an unresolved Oedipus complex. So, in both cases, you must be examined. Now tell me, have you ever considered murdering your father?

- To murder my father? What's the point? Sir, he's already dead.

- Ah! Yes, I'm referring to it before he died.

- No way, sir.

- Sonny, don't lie to me. Didn't his death make you feel better?

- Is it better? When he was alive, things weren't so bad. He was, after all, cool. A wonderful father. I was devastated by his death...

- I see. You had no idea that when he died, he made you happier...

- Fake news! I apologise, sir. Hem... I object. As it appears, you're accusing me of parricide. Anyway, you're accusing me of something I can't even fathom. I object. It is unjust. I DID NOT MURDER MY FATHER!

- I never stated that you did. I was only curious about your reactions when he died. That's beside the point. You should know that the subconscious has its own ways. We all murdered or fantasised about murdering our fathers in order to discover and confirm our personalities. It's the same for you, but don't be concerned; it's only symbolic.

I wondered if it wasn't one of his ruses to

catch me.

- Sir, I am not a murderer. I never killed or even considered killing anyone. Furthermore, I am a faithful man, and such thoughts are grave sins. I don't want to end up in hell because of a symbolic mishmash.

He took a breather.

- So... All right! You persuaded me. You undoubtedly did not inherit your father's bright side. Forget about it all. Anyway, I'm not asking you to do a difficult task.

- I'm your man, sir.

- You will just sit behind a desk and record the title and code number of the book, as well as the borrower's name, on the register. It would be best if you also kept the environment clean and tidy. Is it a challenge?

- No, sir. I know I can accomplish it.

He scribbled on my file and pressed a buzzer on his desk. The helper entered after the gate opened for a brief moment. The shrink handed him a sheet and told him to take me to the library.

- He's the right man for the job.

Then, turning to face me, he said:

- Good luck, Bassam.

I stepped up and thanked him profusely. But before we could even shake hands, the helper - a gorilla similar to the one I'd left outside - yanked me away. Then I realised I hadn't asked about my pay. But it was obvious that the new job had to be gratifying enough following a successful financial career. I won't sweat like a damned until I know they'll pay me adequately. My fiancée, who is ready to get married, would be shocked if she found out what is happening here. "You, a banking professional, how dare you to accept working for peanuts?" She would be outraged. Who will stand up to her? Not me!

So, while in the antechamber, I told the attendant I wanted to return.

- For what purpose?

He said this while scowling suspiciously.

-I neglected to ask him about my...um... ahe m...my... honorarium.

- Your... what exactly?

- That's my pay, brother. I'm talking about what I'm meant to get out of the job.

- Are you sure?

- I'm serious, of course.

Unexpectedly, the man burst out laughing as if he had just heard the best joke of the day. As a result, he presented me with the horrible sight of his dark, damaged teeth and a portion of his ravaged palate. He then abruptly stopped chuckling, but his eyes narrowed, and his low jaw vibrated as he spat:

- Now look, the fucking banker! You've caused enough havoc since you fucked up your nasty facade. So, piss off before I go crazy and do something stupid. Is it clear enough?

Oh my God! I could tell it wasn't my day.

Because the debate was forbidden, I whispered an apology and exited.

The assistant called the black guard, Mahmoud, and informed him that I had been assigned to the library. The latter scoffed at me and snapped mockingly:

- He? Why? The cretin hasn't even spent 24 hours in jail!

- It's a command, said the assistant.

- Ah! So, I see... (Then, in a private tone, perhaps assuming I wasn't paying attention, he added:) Is he one of them?

- I'm not sure, honestly, responded the assistant.

- He must! Those who are assigned to such tasks have already been punished, you know. But the son of a bitch over here is still detained, and no one knows if he will ever appear in court!

- No one, but...

- Yeah! But, as you say. But we must exercise

caution. I'm not ruling anything out. The bastard might be One of them.

I could see myself being a complicated issue for them. I was about to yell, "I'm not one of them!" if that would help. But, in the end, I changed my mind. Wait, man, I told myself. As the therapist put it, if you killed your father without even knowing it, you might as well be one of them and never know it. Consider it.

My subconscious began to erupt into deep waters at that point. It is ready to swallow me up like a huge hydra if I do not correctly interpret the coded message in a strange hieroglyph. Meanwhile, the two men continued their conversation:

- I've bullied him a little, admitted the assistant, sneakily looking at me. The bastard remained silent. I'm concerned he's deceiving us.

- Ah! Did you? Beware. Isn't that a tired trick? You know how they get to this location, but you never know if they're spying on the inmates or on us. Fucking hidden enterprise! Who, after all, is sending them?

- Please keep your voice down. They're everywhere, said the assistant, and it's unclear whether they're pals. Don't you remember Bourisha?

- I do. Before he went, the jerk trashed the place.

- Yes, he did cause your friend's removal, Hamma, didn't he?

The black man sighed heavily and looked at me sidelong before stating:

- Hamma has been in the desert since then, and that cretin of Bourisha has been appointed to our Paris Embassy! What a crazy world!

- Yes, but raping a cop was a bad decision. Hamma carried it out. He fucked a fucking government spy! That was not very wise of him.

- I agree, but who knew who was who by then?

- Ha! That is the question, and it is for this reason that the jerk over there must be dealt with with caution.

The assistant looked at me with interest as he stated this. He even blinked at me as if I were an accomplice. Perhaps he smirked as well, but I didn't respond to his hypocritical snake-like smile for fear of provoking him further. I wasn't sure, but it sounded like the bastard they'd handle with caution was me. I didn't like it, and even though I didn't know who that Bourisha was, I mistook several innuendoes directed at me. However, I soon dismissed this notion because I could never be one of them. In any case, who are they referring to? I replayed it in my thoughts over and over. I recognise that I may be a separate and distinguished individual. Even my new name - or barcode, if you want - is far higher than one. Okay, then! I can't be one or both because I'm one zero zero seven and don't know who the they of them represented! I was satisfied. I could easily breathe. My love of statistics and accurate accounting drew me out of another bad affair. Mahmoud snatched my elbow, putting a halt to my ratiocination.

- All right, the banker. Hurry up. Are you sleeping?

- Sir, yes. Of course, I mean no. Will we be going to the library?

- No, we're not, he yelled. Not with all the nasty little bugs trailing behind you.

- What bugs, sir? I don't have any.

- You say that, but you're not fooling me. We know everything there is to know about you, and look here, man, no shit! I'll keep an eye out for you. Did you comprehend that you have nothing to do over here?

- I appreciate your acknowledgement, sir.

- Close your fucking trap. You scumbag! Stupid shithead!

I chose not to respond. The poor man was

unhappy and irritable. It was fruitless to argue with him. Perhaps he mistook me for someone else. I'm not sure why they're all so irritable. Some people have forgotten themselves to the extent of addressing me as if I were the footman! It's pretty disappointing. What the hell do they think they're doing? The black guard and his aide are almost certainly conspiring and preparing something heinous. I can sense it. It is obvious that they dislike me.

Nonetheless, because I am not their subordinate, I owe solely to my supervisor, Mister Aroussi, who is also present. I need to find a way to welcome him. Perhaps he had already sensed my presence by this point. If he had, he would have been perplexed as to why I had not yet talked to him. On the other hand, even as a library clerk, I believe I owe obedience to the shrink who employed me, not the assistant or the black guard. In the order of the... hem!... Let's be clear: the prison hierarchy, the two men must not be higher than I am. So why should I follow them? If I do, it is because I am a good person. However, I am not oblivious to the fact that they would commit trespassing if I were to be too accommodating. In this life, one must be steadfast in their ideals without becoming too hard or soft. The middle ground is the best option. That is one of my favourite maxims. Regardless of what my blockhead angels think of the question, I consider myself a good Muslim. As back as I can remember, I've always lived in the centre of everything, if not the heart or the nucleus. So, like the bank, I inhabit the centre of the modern universe. Nowadays, all roads go to the bank rather than Rome! With all due respect to the Vatican, the bank has seized control of religion in the hearts of the devout. This is also true for Muslims. It is our new Mecca, and we are all pilgrims in this system, even though we are perfectly aware that our faith forbids certain activities.

But who knows? It is self-evident that banks' interests are like flesh and blood to the body. What's the big deal? Are we going to be the exception to the rule? That would not be acceptable to us. I know exactly what I'm talking about. There is only one banking system on our planet, and there is no room for another. (But here I am again, digressing and nosing about religion, which is not my intention. Let's remove the final paragraph from the report).

Chapter Five

I strolled down the long corridor with my black guard (and two phantom angels), crossing the courtyard where the police vans were stationed. Then we reached a slightly smaller area, and I noticed individuals standing in a row beside the wall. The guard motioned to them with his black finger and said:

- Go. You'll need to see a hairdresser after you've finished showering.

I was ready to say that I hadn't had time to bring my toiletries or any clothing to change out of my crumpled suit. Still, I held back as I peered at the gorilla and noted its grin. I walked right up to the row. My quiet was undeniably more potent than any outcry. The gorilla was aware of it. That's why it disappeared. It has taken a step back! As a result, I won the first round! And knock!

THAT TIME, I DID NOT make the same mistake. I stood up quietly at the back of the row. I never sought to be the first to enter the shrink's office. I am both obedient and disciplined. My daily existence has been so meticulously planned that one could claim, without exaggeration, that Bassam Bourasin is Big Ben! Although some cops are not as trustworthy as they should be, I should have made a good cop. I even knew one who would steal radio cassettes from the vehicles he was supposed to watch over. To make ends meet, he would sell them illegally on the market. Once apprehended, he sold the stolen goods to the wrong man. It was another cop who was looking into the situation. Needless to say, the robber was burned. The detective, one of my customers, relayed the incident to me. He was sorry, but he had to report his colleague's misbehaviour. What a shame! Worse. When the thief-cop realised he was dealing with a detective, he attempted to bribe him. He provided the radio cassette as a gift, which exacerbated his situation. And I recognised him when he described him to me. I had dealt with him when I purchased a used tape for my car. It was the same man: a traffic cop during the day and a merchant of stolen things on weekends. He was an expert in radio cassettes, CDs, video and camera systems for all types of automobiles. Then I realised I had purchased stolen goods. I was ready to confess to the investigator when I decided to hold my tongue. It's not that I'm dishonest, but it wasn't my problem. The implications could be severe: if I admit to buying a stolen item from the same individual disguised in civilian vacation attire, I will be summoned to the police station, if not as an accomplice, then as a witness. Furthermore, I would be forced to return the items I had paid for, and who would reimburse me? The cops? That's hard to believe. So, why should I give up something I paid for with my money? Life is not that simple. However, if the police adequately compensated its agents, they would not resort to thievery and gangsterism to make ends meet. Take a look at what's going on right now:

People are losing their sense of security. One never knows if a traffic warden who stops you on the road is an honest man or a masked thief. But where are we going if everyone begins thinking like this? That is why I believe a good citizen who loves his nation and is loyal to its Administration should not have two jobs simultaneously and in the same area. Really! You cannot serve two masters at the same time. Who made this statement? I don't mind, but he was correct. One of the two masters would eventually be duped.

Furthermore, if more officers start stealing and swindling, professional thieves will be in short supply sooner or later. Authentic and honest thieves would not tolerate that unjust and imbalanced rivalry. As a result, they would be forced to change their business or relocate. The first approach would exacerbate the country's difficult and time-consuming unemployment problem. The second would aggravate the problem of irregular emigration among Europeans. As free market proponents, we must foster competitiveness when the two sides are on equal footing at the outset. However, because the would-be thieves among the officers already have a job, they would take unfair advantage. Their inexperience would undermine both professions. More cops would be in jail, and fewer professional thieves would be on the streets, for it is evident that an amateur would end up in prison shortly. A professional ruffian, on the other hand, would depart the country, concerned by the unrivalled emulation.

However, when one thinks about it closely, it is impossible not to recognise our police's wit and intelligence. There are more opportunities to imprison an amateur thief than a professional, and our officers know where they would end up. This is most likely a huge sacrifice they are making at their own risk and hazard for the sake - without a doubt - of their oath: to rid our streets of professional ruffians.

That's the secret!

This, I dare to say, is a very patriotic act. The cop willing to take the risk, sacrificing his free time for the sake of the population, should be encouraged to study the tough job of a thief, cutthroat, gangster, and similar businesses. We should also give him the National Hero medal.

Let us be clear:

The unlucky cop apprehended by a fellow cop in the marketplace while attempting to smuggle his stolen goods is a Hero, though he is unaware of it. His coworker doesn't either. He should get the Order Of High Merit because his action prevented a real burglar from stealing those radio cassettes. If he hadn't taken such precautions, the professional burglars would have stolen the same items.

I did not tell the detective about these ideas or the reasonable conclusion I had come to. I instead asked:

- What happened to the police officer?

- He's in jail.

How awful! Even willful ignorance of the man's abilities couldn't make me indifferent to him. I was very moved by the story. I could not feel anything but sympathy for the innocent bystander of social ignorance. He did not act to make ends meet, I am sure. But his sense of right and wrong made him want to stop bad people from breaking into the cars of his fellow citizens. Is that really so hard to get? It's easy, though: If you can fool the thieves and stop them from doing what they usually do, it's like pulling the rug out from under them and forcing them to be unemployed. This is called "preemption" in the world of strategy. Yes, sir. Such work comes with risks and a sense of giving up something.

Once the hero was caught with his hand in the bag, he would be fired and told to stay away from the police. He would also have to spend many hard years in jail. Also, the guy wasn't acting selfishly when he made honest people like me pay half or even less of the real price for electronics. His kindness, bravery, friendliness, and willingness to give up things are evident. We should support, encourage, and reward the would-be thieves, thugs, and gangsters in our National Police who try to be like him.

(Well. Let's forget that last sentence about would-be thieves, thugs, and gangsters in ou r...etc.)

Chapter Six

I was making my way carefully towards the Hammam's entrance. The courtyard's excessive exposure to daylight was quite uncomfortable. Although only two of the four seasons are observed here, the arrival of spring signals the start of the year. The rest is just a euphemism for winter or summer. My flower pots in 'Ouja must be drying out by now. And the poor canary must be wondering why I haven't replaced its water or filled its small recipient with seeds, as I used to. But, most importantly, it may be desiring sugar.

I am sorry, canary, but I was not forewarned. I had no idea I was so desperately needed in the... Capital. I didn't have time to pack properly, so I had to go without my pyjamas and toothbrush. This is the very first time in my life that I have embarked on such an excursion. The two men who accompanied me to the city were in such a hurry that you'd think the devil himself was hot on their heels. They arrived in the afternoon and hammered on the door so loudly I was scared the bank had been looted or burned down. I had settled into my favourite couch to watch a live TV show. I hadn't expected any visitors and was astonished to find those two angry and tense men when I opened the door. One of them asked:

- Are you Bassam Bourasin?

I noted he hadn't even said Mister, as anyone polite would, and I didn't like his expression.

- Yes, I said. May I ask what...?

He cut me off, saying, "Police!"

My heart was pounding wildly, and I managed to retain my cool and said:

- This is a wonderful honour, gentlemen. Would you please come inside my humble home and join me for a drink?

- We don't have time! You'll enjoy your drink in a particularly welcoming hotel. So put on your clothes and follow us.

I afterwards regretted my haste to leave my flat without taking some measures. The truth is that I candidly assumed I had been invited to join them for a drink at the local hotel. I couldn't believe we were going to travel to the Capital straight immediately, and it wasn't until we were well out of 'Ouja that I dared to ask:

- Where are we heading, gentlemen? May I inquire?

One of them laughed, and the driver responded:

- Don't you know it yet?

- If I did, I wouldn't ask.

- Didn't we tell you about a drink in a great hotel?

- Ah! Yes, absolutely. But when we left 'Ouja, I noticed no hotel nearby. The man next to me on the back bench stopped laughing and added:

- You're going to the most wonderful hotel in the country. You're very fortunate, man!

- Okay, then.

However, I was unconvinced. Before entering the car, the two men handcuffed me. I let them do it without saying anything. I didn't want to startle my neighbours, who were usually watching. Nothing seemed more important to me than my reputation in town. As a result, while quietly complying, I tried to avoid violence and scandal. I could even understand the two men's uneasiness. With all the criminal attempts mentioned in the headlines and terrorists lurking in the shadows, the police are having a difficult time.

Nonetheless, I held my tongue and said nothing. After all, if I couldn't feel safe and secure while being guarded by the cops, where could I? Even if I did not enjoy my time in the nation's capital, I could not deny that its hotels are more appealing and luxurious than the modest inn where I usually stay.

'OUJA IS NOT A TOWN; it is not even touristic like the southern shore. That is why, if properly managed, a single inn is sufficient. I occasionally sit at the coffee shop with a small drink, playing cards with friends or random visitors. In the village, I am as well-known as Coke, not because everyone knows everyone other in such a small town, but because I enjoy people's trust as a bank clerk. However, if they trust me, it is most likely because they believe their money is safer in our hands than in theirs, which is undeniably true. Such assurance is the genuine capital of our company. Any bank employee would agree. This dictum should be engraved in gold letters on the front door of any respectable financial institution.

Mr Aroussi, our director, used to say this when he met with our most significant clients. Our community may be small, but it's home to some interesting and, dare I say it, wealthy patrons. Our records show that they have many accounts in our vault. Funds that would make us feel very proud if we could reveal their value. But doing so would violate the confidentiality we're sworn to uphold.

Banking is a remarkable industry. Whereas other trades thrive by publicising their transactions' quantity, size, and number, we do the opposite since we are bound by confidentiality. A bank's popularity and trustworthiness will rise in proportion to how discreet it is with its customers' information. That puts bankers and bank tellers squarely opposing politicians. The more trusted and popular a politician is at the start, the more he talks and forgets to keep his promises... (I'm sliding down a perilous slope. Not only did I imply that banks are in opposition, but I also dared to equate bankers to politicians! So, I'm going to repress this delirium as well. I must produce a clean report because I'm trying to mount a good defence. But now I see I'm fishing in troubled waters and sinking!)

SINCE WE'RE TALKING about water, I should mention that the Hammam is not what I imagined. More specifically, it has nothing to do with a genuine Hammam.

I walked into a large, dark, nearly smoky room that was moist with steam. I noticed individuals jostling naked or half-naked beneath the dashing waters running from showers hanging above their heads as soon as I could see through the bleak fog. I stood there staring at the strange scene, dumbfounded. Nearby, some individuals were dressed or undressed on a long wooden bench. When I was debating whether or not a reputable bank clerk should have spoken with such a rabble, I felt a strong hand clasp my shoulder, and a gruff voice boomed in my ear:

- What the fuck are you waiting for, mosquito?

I turned my head, my hands interlocked.

A massive bald head with two black eyes

gleamed from a face so horribly damaged that I initially mistook it for a mask rather than a real person. Monstrously, twisted, and crushed that nose. Two lengthy scars crisscrossed the mouth, clearly the gruesome marks of a knife. Seeing that unyielding Hollywood monster made me freeze, so I mumbled an apology and ran away. Where, though? Frankenstein himself had reached out and grabbed my shoulder, pulling me in.

- What are your plans?

His bright eyes were not all good. When I realised I was no longer safe. I yelled for the black guard to come to save me. However, I was unable to get a single syllable out. My voice had failed me miserably. I've never been a fan of scary films. Many years ago, when I saw Dracula and Frankenstein, I had to fight my desire to sleep for two nights in a row.

I could be more robust and agile. Unfortunately, I had little chance of successfully repelling the beast because mother nature had not been kind to me. That's completely insane. Even though I do not consider myself a coward, I lack the heroic qualities necessary to succeed. He could easily knock me over with one hand if he wanted to. He was easily three times as tall and wide as I was. He wore a T-shirt over pants rolled up at the calves, and his bare feet dangled in a puddle of filthy water on the floor.

He examined me as a scientist would examine the movements of a wiggling creature with fascination and wonder. I was sweating profusely and gasping for air. Then, much to his enjoyment and my hate, he cuddled me up against his chest and squeezed me so hard I almost passed out. His rotten teeth shone with a smug glee as he laughed. His breath carried the pungent odour of cigarettes, garlic, and other putrid substances. Of course, I was taken aback by such a warm welcome, but I had to work desperately for air. By the end, I realised it was all for nought. It made me uncomfortable, so I gave up trying.

-Are you a troublemaker? he asked.

-No...Not... Not at all... ssssssssssssssssssssss ssssssssssssssss...sir! I stumbled.

- Are you a gangster?

-You... You're....err...miss...misses...taken...

- Me? Mistaken? Do you dare offend me? Fuckkkkkkkking mosquito!

I attempted to lull him in some way:

- I did... I did not...I did not...mean it, sir. I...I am...you...your...humble...servant!

- Serve my ass! You filthy son of a bitch! Didn't you pretend I was mistaken? So, yeah, I'm a jerk! That's what you're saying?

The small brawl had taken a hazardous turn. The monster's arm tightened around my waist. Then I was squished down like a worm on a stone. I attempted diplomacy once more:

- You aren't a jerrrrk. I...I...I aaaaam..... Not yyyyyoouu, Nnnnn!

He loosened his grip. I took a breath. Nonetheless, he did not release me.

I exclaimed:

- I am just a simple bank employee, sir. I'm not trying to offend you. How could I do it? You're...so...so...

- So, so what?

I wanted to yell: "So vile! So ugly! So disgusting!..." But I mumbled modestly:

- So gracious, sir! I feel incredibly honoured and blessed to have met you!

Then he let me go. I regained my footing. Even though I wasn't aware of it, I was hovering above the ground during the catching game. While I was trying to gather my thoughts, he asked:

- What did you say you are?

I trembled, expecting the worst. Was the horrible thing plotting another placement? I looked at him, puzzled, but he didn't move. He could have been offended if I told him I worked as a bank clerk again. It makes no dif-ference if he is a big guy. He is undeniably sensitive, if not hypersensitive. The least hint of anything outside of his world may be dis-astrous. He may have suffered from a lack of maternal compassion as a child. I once read that abused children grow up quiet, sensitive, introverted, and unable to function in society. Perhaps even spiteful against it. The more I looked at Frankenstein, the more I realised this was his personality. But, as sympathetic as I am to the destitute and wretched, I am not Mother Theresa. I don't have the calling or the desire to be his prey either. He definitely needs his mother more than he needs me.

On the other hand, there was a real possi-bility that if I lied to him, he might bully and molest me even more. He may have heard me and was only testing my credibility. So, in the end, I resolved to tell the truth, regardless of the repercussions. I was conscious that I was playing a game. To be sure, not on the stock exchange, but on the volatile rascal's stock feelings.

- All right, sir.

I explained that I work as a bank clerk... a very modest bank employee. He sounded as if he was laughing at it! Thankfully, he smirked. Then I realised I'd won.

- Did you mention you worked as a bank teller? So you work at a bank, correct?

He was almost overjoyed. His expression had changed to that of Christopher Columbus discovering America!

- Sir, yes. A bank clerk is a person who works for a bank! That's what I do!

His response was unexpected. He appeared to be ecstatic. He lightly tapped me on the shoulder as if I were an old friend. Then, in an enthusiastic outpouring, he asked:

- Why haven't you mentioned it since the morning, man? We're friends! Don't you realise it? We're relatives, cousins, brothers, come with me, guy! Kiss Uncle Salih.

A KISS? I WAS REVOLTED at the prospect of kissing that terrible face of nightmares, me, who used to be so delicate and diversified in my choices! As a child, whenever someone kissed me on the Islamic holidays, I would rush to the restroom to wash my face! I'm so disgusted with such trivialities that I can't remember ever kissing anyone since I was a kid. Not even my mother or my fiancée.

Regarding the latter, Allah is a witness. I never even attempted to touch her. Except for the day of our wedding. Then I had no choice but to slide the ring onto her finger. That happened five years ago. Whenever we were alone in her parents' house at the time, she would try to get closer to me. But she was so awkward that we never kissed. In any case, my values prevent such behaviour.

Once, in the dimness of a movie theatre, I felt her warm hand firmly grasp mine. It was close to panic time for me. I assumed she was terrified because of the violence on the screen. She was likewise unaware of her younger brother, who sat alongside her. It seemed prudent to retract my hand after some consideration. Still, she didn't notice because she was focused on the movie. I felt relieved after that. I could breathe normally without my blood heating up from excitement. However, she did not say her last word. She hesitated for a second, then tried again, this time with greater zeal. Her left leg was stuck to mine then, and her fingers were ploughing my thigh, hopelessly groping for something they didn't dare touch. It was too much for me to endure. To say I was ashamed is far below the truth. She turned me on, and I felt like a hot dog. I was gasping for air and on the edge of collapse. She was oblivious to everything around her: her brother, my hot blood, the public, morals, religion, family, and village! Such hedonism was intolerable. Scandalising!

I had the impression that hundreds of eyes were no longer focused on the big screen but on her little fingers, methodically, rapturously rubbing my thigh. It was so daring! I anticipated and anticipated the worst. I needed to figure out how to avoid it without insulting her. It was a difficult task, but I had no alternative. I didn't want the whole town gossiping and screaming about our public displays of salacious profligacy.

Furthermore, the situation in the sphere of operations, if I may say so, was rapidly approaching a peak. I didn't like the direction it was headed. It was a perilous incline. I quickly realised I had a massive erection and had no idea what to do about it. As a result, I reacted gently yet firmly. I took her hand away. Then, pretending to answer nature's call, I dashed to the restroom. I locked the door behind me, unzipped and went wild with fingers and eyes and darkness and movies and fingers moving high low high low high low high low high high high hiiiiiiiiiiiiiiiiiiiiiiiiiiiiiiiiiiiiiiiiiiiiiiiiiiiiiiiiiiiiiiiiiiiiiii.. ....!

I returned slowly, relaxed but guilty, and sat between my fiancée and her brother. Since that day, I've been able to keep the brother between us whenever we go to the movies. As a result, there is no excitement, panic, or...

HOWEVER, UNTIL I GAVE into the impossible, I couldn't address the issue of kissing

Frankenstein. I lingered, paused, delayed, and circled the pot, but I knew I had to do it, that I was going to do it, and that I... I gathered my courage, which was desperately needed at the time. I hobbled forward and, on my tiptoes, closed my eyes (if only to avoid seeing what I was doing) and stretched, stretched, stretched in vain. Because he was so much taller than me, I could not kiss him on the cheek. Thankfully, he rescued me from further humiliation. He bent over and dropped his head so I could kiss his horrifying scar, and I did.

What needed to be done was completed. Baa! Forgive me, God. I thought my life was over. He patted me on the back and said:

- Good kid!" The time has come for us to start working together.

Me? Trading with the Monster Man? Holy crap! The day I accept it, I will almost certainly be uninspired or insane. What the hell happened? I've already worked with people far more human than that freak, and I've seen the results. It's not exactly brilliant right now. So, I know what would happen if I was in the same boat as that repulsive creature. We'd go down together to the bottom of this horrible earth or swim to shore only to discover a scaffold ready to snap our necks! In my opinion, this is the only possible result of such a ridiculous coalition. Obviously, I was not prepared to carry on with such a pointless exchange. I am not a coward; I have declared as much. I'd succeeded by taking calculated chances, but I recognised my limits. There is nothing beyond them but no man's land, prison, exile, and the gallows. Well, I'm already in jail, which is not pleasant. What occurred? Have I gone too far? This appears to be the case. I am, therefore, as guilty as Mr Aroussi, who preceded me to this honourable State guesthouse.

Nonetheless, I couldn't understand clearly what my crime was. When I could, I assisted others. I only made some people more prosperous than they were before they came to me. But I'll get into that later.

For now, all I could think about was hurrying to the shower to wash away any traces of that horrific kiss. I was no longer debating whether it was appropriate for a bank clerk to associate with the filthy mob. I've always despised promiscuity. That was not because I am a serial snub but because I am concerned about my bank's reputation. If it helped, I would deal with some customers while wearing gloves. However, it is prohibited. I had to be nice to everyone, even those I couldn't frame since some stupid blockheads required warmth and solicitude in our dealings! And now I was expected to act similarly with the customers of this particular house. Well! After all, promiscuity with the rabble clamouring beneath the showers might be more enjoyable than this repulsive tête-à-tête with Frankenstein.

I told him not to hurt him in a sweet tone:

- We'll do whatever you want, but please let me shower now.

I decided it would be better to include: - Mr Mahmud is waiting for me outside.

- Who is that jerk?

- The guard, sir, the large black guard.

- Ah! You mean the colour of my balls, which is dark?

- All right, sir. That is the correct one.

- What exactly is he waiting for? Do you have any kinship? Is he a relative, a brother-in-law, or something else?

- No, sir.

He became upset when I did not respond:

- And so what? Is he your bedfellow? Who is banging whom?

I was taken aback. The shock I felt was incredible. Dismayed to hear such hateful nonsense. For a moment, I seriously considered charging at him, sticking my fangs into his ear, and biting him so firmly, persistently, and mercilessly that I would rip it right out of his ugly skull. I looked down, and there he was, face muddied with blood and yelling and screaming and rolling around on the ground and moving up to me. It made me really vengeful. I've been able to laugh at his silly jokes like they're nothing and put up with his sleazy, prison humour. Nonetheless, I was not to take such suggestive remarks at face value.

Just who the hell do you think you are? Superman? I felt like I might scream. But I kept my cool and didn't let it get the best of me. Simply put, it was an attempt at cheap provocation. Was I supposed to make a beeline for the sneaky trap? No. The fight was too one-sided, to be fair. Before I could even get a word in edgewise, he'd knock me out cold, and that would be that for me and his shindig. He has the wrong impression of me; I am not

as dimwitted as he thinks I am. Cold lunch is
the finest way to get even with someone. You'll
need some time to stir it up and let it cool
down. So I shot back:

- Sir, I have nothing to do with him. But he is
in charge of maintaining order and discipline
here. So he might be wondering why I'm lin-
gering in the shower...

- Is that it?

- Absolutely, sir.

- Well! You should be aware that I am
the FUCKING IN CHARGE OF THE
BLOODY ORDER over here, and your black-
ish can show his baboon ass elsewhere. (He
stopped before adding:) Now you can shower.

He added, "Go now," as I thanked him profusely. "We'll discuss business later."

Doing business with me was quickly becoming one of his obsessions! But it wasn't all bad.
I reminded myself. Okay, never mind. I can get
something out of this if I can exploit his hope

and delay it indefinitely cleverly. I can secure safety with little more than word of mouth and assurances. The people of this place appear to hold him in high esteem if not outright fear. In addition, he did not appear intimidated by the security personnel. Perhaps the converse is also true. Because it's not often that people breathe a sigh of relief at the sight of a genuine Frankenstein lurking around.

Nonetheless, I replied not out of opportunism but out of common sense. I am a man who adheres to high moral standards. My life is generally orderly and neat. I never improperly abused or deceived others or took advantage of their kindness. As a bank clerk, I couldn't stand up to honest profit. That would be a slap in the face to the principles of my honourable profession. In Frankenstein's situation, however, it would be foolish and dangerous not to take advantage of his desire to dominate him. There is a solid reason for this: plainly, if his energy is not effectively channelled and contained, he may be somewhat dangerous - to himself and others. As a result, I hope to do something instructive, moral, and even altruistic. Before I stripped naked, all I managed to say was:

-You're making a bargain, sir. If you take my advice, this will be one of the best deals you've ever made.

I truly meant it.

I folded my clothes, placed them on the bench, and proceeded to the shower. However, there was no room for me. I had to wait until one of the guys agreed to let me take over. Then I recognised how beneficial my recent collaboration with Franken had been! He dashed toward me as soon as he noticed me waiting and yanked one of the men from the showers. Then he yelled:

- Come along, the banker! This is your battery!

I walked quietly and, rather embarrassed,

placed myself under the lukewarm splashing water to thank him for the quick service. At the same time, the harassed man stepped back, casting poisoned stares at me from beneath the white film of soap foaming and bubbling over his face. I thought it would be polite to apologise because he seemed so angry. He did not complain or react in any way, but he was most certainly unhappy. So I apologised:

- I am sorry for the inconvenience...

I attempted to demonstrate my goodwill. I even cracked a smile. But the enraged man remained motionless! On the contrary, he was as quiet as a rug!

IT WOULD APPEAR THAT I have not yet exhausted the benefits of my new relationship.

When a hand reached out and gave me some soap, the shower finally became enjoyable. After I used the soap twice, someone brought me a shampoo bottle. While someone bathed my head, they rubbed my back with a towel. I felt like a king being served, and when the friendly friction subsided, I turned to thank the guy who had offered to assist me. To my amazement, it was the man who had been so abruptly replaced. Both pain and pleasure hit me simultaneously. For my part, as a man of peace, I didn't want to so much as give somebody the germ of an idea to start a grudge against me from day one. But the gentleman's generosity won me over.

Despite my current predicament, I have no known adversaries. I'm afraid it is an arrest. However, I must concede that unseen and powerful adversaries, including my two guardian angels, manufactured it. It's a conspiracy. I am in a good position to notice this.

My professional success and loyal dedication to the bank and my boss, Mr Aroussi, led to this risky connection with inmates and troublemakers. Those bitter about my accomplishment will likely have their way within the Administration. They were able to get my powerful boss and me down here. They have long arms and probably very long legs as well... Anyway, they are longer and stronger than mine. Yet I don't want to pin the blame on the Administration completely. God save me from such craziness! I remain loyal to the Administration of our country, which I consider the most intelligent in the world. Without question, I say IN THE WORLD. (Well done, Sonny. Continue like this. I'm your good angel adviser).

However, remember that even in a basket full of healthy eggs, two or three - if not many more - may be tipsy and indigestible. But it is too early to provide a thorough analysis of the issue.

It would be more prudent to proceed step by
step because I aim to be completely honest in
telling all that had happened since and before
I arrived in the Capital.

BEFORE I GOT OUT OF the shower, I
thanked the man who had chafed my back and
apologised again. I felt it would be best to in-
troduce myself so we might become acquaint-
ed under different circumstances, as I was not
indifferent to his distress. I extended my hand
and said:

- Bank teller Bassam Bourasin here, your obedient servant.

I expected him to tell me his name and position and shake my hand. Instead, he looked at
me as though taken aback by the disparity in

my demeanour. Despite his girth, the man was not much taller than me.

- Go fuck yourself, you motherfucker hurly burly monkey!

His odd eyes narrowed as he spat his words coldly.

Shocked? I was. I mean, who wouldn't be? That's some seriously nefarious talk, full of explicit malice. Certainly an oddity! Irrelevant! Impolite!

I couldn't say anything since I felt warm and fuzzy towards him. In other words, he had no intention of shaking my hand. So I just let it go. As losses go, it wasn't too bad. I was upset nonetheless but for an entirely different reason. I was so disheartened that I forgot about myself and stared stupidly at him. Next, his oddly lit eyes flared with fire, and he growled:

- If you don't piss off right now, I will crush your bloody face of a damned monkey! Have I made myself clear?

BLOODY FACE OF A DAMNED mon-
key? Who's that? Me? He surely hadn't looked
at himself in the mirror since the deluge.
He was far more repulsive than the genuine
Frankenstein, not the phantom lost around
here. The latter's ugliness is, I'm sure, factitious
and may be arranged correctly. With the assistance of an aesthetic surgeon, he may emerge
as handsome as a movie star. He would not,
however, be Valentino. But if you remove his
scars, position his nose in the middle of his
face, and let him wear a wig, he'll look virtually
as natural as any other person.

Regarding the former, I honestly believe that
even with the assistance of a skilled surgeon, he
would not emerge with a bearable appearance.

I'm talking about something that resembles a human, not an animal. The poor devil was doomed indefinitely. And he was completely unaware of it! I'm afraid I'm speaking of an ontogenetic failure. I did look it up in the dictionary. (Ontogenetic: from ontogenesis, is the origination and development of an organism, both physical and psychological.) His mother must have slept with a horse, donkey, or beast to produce such a wild miracle.

To begin with, he has the exact head he should not have, as it was fashioned in the shape of an empty bottle tossed on the wrong side. Second, his large ears were perched obliquely on each side of his head, ready to fly away. Third, unlike most mortals, his eyes were not set up straight on a vertical line. I believe one of them, the left, was much higher than the second! I wasn't even sure I saw it correctly. As I kept staring at him to ensure I wasn't hallucinating, he became agitated and reacted aggressively. It's understandable! When gifted with such kind of shopwindow, one must blame one's mother all day and night! Nonetheless, I believe he has a unique opportunity to produce himself in a circus arena without learning any special expertise. He'd make a living by showing off his amazing eyes to the public.

Not to mention his ready-to-fly outboard ears and the upside-down bottle on his shoulders. The poor man! Despite this, he dares to call me the monkey! Well! It's hardly an insult coming from his mouth, I suppose. I know I'm not who he made me out to be. I am not as attractive as Valentino, but I am quite okay. I'm a little brownish, with a well-bridged nose, a respectable mouth, two dark eyes - neither more nor less, and symmetric - and two ears sticking to my head with no will to take off. My hair is black, which, I admit, is not wholly original. Nonetheless, it is curled and fluffy, and my features are normal. No scar, no eye higher than the other, and no taking off ears, thanks to Allah and my mother's discerning wisdom!

Then I heard Frankenstein's baritone voice thundering through the room:

- Hey! Zorro! Please relax. He returned your shower; what else do you want?

- He owes me money for the shampoo, soap, and towel he used! The enraged man snapped.

- He'll pay for your grubby soap, muttered Frankenstein. He works as a banker! And if he refuses, I will. Please charge that to my account. Is it all right?

The so-called Zorro quieted down and roared inaudibly. I was thankful to my new partner, who took our agreement seriously. He motioned to someone behind me. A man handed me a dry towel. I wiped the wetness from my body. Life was glorious again.

Chapter Seven

I hadn't yet gotten used to the prison's atmosphere. I don't think I ever will be. But, like any newbie, I couldn't help but notice the anomalies and eccentricities of the location. Which, to the untrained sight, appears both pointless and petty. I will not squander time now that I have been designated library clerk. I plan to document every thrilling tale I hear and every significant or insignificant detail I observe. Everything will go into the revamping report I'll present to the Administration. This is a project I'm working on on my own, something neither the shrink nor the black guard encouraged me to accomplish. As I discovered, writing anything other than letters in jail is even illegal. Any correspondence, whether from the outside or the inside, must be approved by the Administration. I am not breaking the law because my report is also a letter sent to the High - probably the Highest - Authorities in the country. I'll be as quiet and cautious as possible. However, I shall be courteous. I will not use the most vexing nomination of this educational and extremely effective national institution. Instead, I'll keep using the word HOTEL as a label. It is more convenient, aesthetically pleasing, and less taxing on the potential reader (and me!) In any case, it is not a prison. Since our Beloved General President's (BGP) popular coup and military revolution, all liberties have been restored, which means that jails do not exist anymore. We don't have people in prison, just people in State Hotels. Our fellow citizens already got the unparalleled taste of liberty they deserve! However, for their own interest, freedom has been hidden to protect it. I carefully memorise the major speeches of our BGP. I even recommended to my supervisor, Mr Aroussi, to engrave a sentence of the BGP with gold lettering and display it on the front wall of the bank in the main hall. Just across from the entrance so that everyone could enjoy the view. That was a few days after the popular coup of the military revolution (I don't know yet how to describe the historical event). The boss coughed, hesitated, and then said:

- You, Bassam, you'll go far away and much higher, I tell you. It's a fantastic idea! Perfect!

He then provided his orders. The Historical phrase was carried up to the Director's office the same week, tastefully printed and framed. Mr Aroussi called me over the phone. I rushed up to inspect the beauty that had been my idea. When I walked in, the director pointed to the golden frame and asked:

- What do you think of it? In a week, all of the banks in the country would either follow our lead or go out of business! Ha ha ha ha ha ha ha! We have prevailed in both situations. Aren't we the ones who put the notion forward? No asshole would deny it, I assure you. I'll make sure it's extensively publicised in national newspapers as well.

He was grinning. It was one of his most wonderful days. A triumph! And if he thought of giving it full attention in the newspapers - it was a real scoop anyhow! - I did not miss the point: the President - I mean our BGP- is rumoured to be a voracious reader of newspapers and periodicals! Mr Aroussi is a brilliant man. I could only agree with his idea. That was the correct approach to whack hard and high. Nevertheless, I was bothered by something weird. I told him so. He gazed at me, a bit perplexed and said:

- What's the trouble? Is it, not your idea?

- Of course, it is, sir, but look at their mess! They printed the sentence with golden letters, all right! But they missed the crucial point. For I do not see the name of our Beloved General President anywhere! How could the reader know who the source of such wisdom is? What if the clients mistake it for some banal quotation from Plato, Tolstoi, or even Spinoza?

- Spinoza? Oh no, no, for God's sake! Our President must not be confused with one of those guys. Who's that Spinoza anyway? A friend of yours?

- No, sir. I randomly picked up his name in a magazine while working the crosswords.

- Ah! Well! I'd better not know who's the chap in case he turns out to be a conspirator. Anyway, I'll issue directives for the sentence to be reprinted immediately.

It was done. In twenty-four hours, the new golden frame was decorating the front wall of our hall so that no eye could miss it. I congratulated Mr Aroussi when I saw in the national newspapers the following advertisement:

Following His Excellency Mister President of the Republic's historic address, the 'Ouja filial of the National Bank, led by the dynamic Mr Aroussi Mamitu, adopted a new motto. From "Your Confidence Is Our Real Capital," as it once was, to "NO PRISONS IN OUR COUNTRY BUT FREEDOM FOR ALL."

This was derived from the same speech, highlighting and reinforcing the bank's loyalty to our beloved Mister President's insightful thoughts. Mr Mamitu aims to be an example for other banks and organisations to follow.

IT WAS FOLLOWED, BUT not in the way we anticipated.

Mr Aroussi was summoned to the Capital after the advertisement was published. I was told he received a call from the Big Boss's secretary. So he left, most likely assuming the Chairman wanted to congratulate him.

It was the last time I saw him before realising he was a State guest in this institution, just like me!

MORE TO COME... STAY tuned.

Book (2) of The Morning of the Mogul: James Bond in Jail

ABOUT THE AUTHOR

• Writer /Journalist/ Senior Researcher: London

• Published over 30 books and counting (translations not included).

• Authored, co-authored, edited, and published hundreds of daily/ weekly/ monthly briefings, reports and analyses, peer-reviewed articles, monographs, and books, about MENA region and international politics.

• Participated in many international conferences on the panel, as a member of the organising team, or as a journalist.

• Has been involved with the media since his early career, thus serving in different posts: reporter, investigation journalist, copy editor, cultural journalism, political journalism, editorialist, and Executive Editor.

• Translated several books/documents. Also reviewed translations for publishers.

• Member of several academic boards.

• Veteran columnist and commentator for the media.

• Ranking in the top 10%of Authors by all-time Social Science Research Network downloads.

• You can follow him on this website:

https://hichemkaroui.net/

Email:

info@global-east-west.co.uk

www.ingramcontent.com/pod-product-compliance
Lightning Source LLC
Chambersburg PA
CBHW031003210726
48290CB00007B/2454